LET'S LOOK

For Surprises All Around

A Lift-the-Flap Photo Book

By Harold Roth

Grosset & Dunlap · New York

Copyright © 1988 by Harold Roth. Published by Grosset & Dunlap, Inc., a member of The Putnam Publishing Group, New York. All rights reserved. Printed in Singapore. Published simultaneously in Canada. Library of Congress Catalog Card Number: 87-83206   ISBN 0-448-10686-8
A B C D E F G H I J

There are surprises
everywhere, just
waiting to be found.
Let's look all around
and see how many
we can find.

Look at the sky.
There might be a surprise
hiding behind one of those
fluffy white clouds.
Let's look.

Look at the ground.
There's a rock
in the grass.
Let's pick it up.

Look at the
colorful leaves
on this big tree.
Something is hiding
behind them.
Let's move the
branches and see
what it is.

Here is a playground.
But there's no one
climbing on the
wooden beams.

Let's peek inside
the tunnel.

Mmm.
Peanut butter and jelly
make a delicious lunch.
What's for dessert?
Let's open the lunch box
and see.

Peek-a-boo,
peek-a-boo!
Here's another
surprise for you.

Dingdong!
The doorbell is ringing.
Can you guess
who's at the door?

Look at all the balloons
and streamers!

Let's open the doors
and see what's
going on inside.

It's fun to open
birthday presents.
A big, soft puppy
makes a wonderful
birthday surprise!

If you look carefully,
you can find surprises
almost anywhere—
inside, outside,
and all around.